This book belongs to:

WREN

Quiet Bunny's
Many Colors

To Sasha, who is beautiful in every way.

STERLING and the distinctive Sterling logo are registered trademarks of
Sterling Publishing Co., Inc.

Library of Congress Cataloging-in-Publication Data
McCue, Lisa.
  Quiet Bunny's many colors / written and illustrated by Lisa McCue.
    p. cm.
  Summary: Quiet Bunny loves the beautiful colors of springtime in the
forest so much, he wants to change his fur's winter colors.
  ISBN 978-1-4027-7209-2
  [1. Rabbits--Fiction. 2. Color--Fiction. 3. Spring--Fiction. 4.
Individuality--Fiction.] I. Title.
  PZ7.M4784149Quie 2011
  [E]--dc22

                                              2009053323

Lot#:
4 6 8 10 9 7 5
12/12
Published by Sterling Publishing Co., Inc.
387 Park Avenue South, New York, NY 10016
Text © 2010 by Lisa McCue
Illustrations © 2010 by Lisa McCue
Distributed in Canada by Sterling Publishing
c/o Canadian Manda Group, 165 Dufferin Street
Toronto, Ontario, Canada M6K 3H6
Distributed in the United Kingdom by GMC Distribution Services
Castle Place, 166 High Street, Lewes, East Sussex, England BN7 1XU
Distributed in Australia by Capricorn Link (Australia) Pty. Ltd.
P.O. Box 704, Windsor, NSW 2756, Australia

Printed in Canada

Sterling ISBN 978-1-4027-7209-2

For information about custom editions, special sales, premium and
corporate purchases, please contact Sterling Special Sales
Department at 800-805-5489 or specialsales@sterlingpublishing.com.

Quiet Bunny's Many Colors

Lisa McCue

STERLING

New York / London

Quiet Bunny loves springtime in the forest.

He loves the warm sun on his soft little nose.
He loves the tickly new grass between his toes.

Most of all, he loves the beautiful colors.

One sunny spring morning, Quiet Bunny sat in a field of dandelions, watching a butterfly flutter about. A mother duck waddled past with her ducklings.

The sun is yellow, the flowers and the butterfly are yellow,
and even the little ducklings are yellow, thought Quiet Bunny.
Yellow is a spring color.

He looked down at his fur. *I am the color of winter. White like the snow
and brown like the trees. I would like to be a spring color. I would like
to be yellow!*

But how?

Something sticky dripped on Quiet Bunny's head. Honey!

Quiet Bunny touched the sticky honey with his paw.
He eyed the puffy yellow dandelions all around him.

Quiet Bunny got an idea.

"Now I am yellow!"
he said.

Quiet Bunny felt quite beautiful. He hopped through the forest, hoping someone would notice him. Soon enough, bees came buzzing. Their buzzing was so noisy that Quiet Bunny didn't hear the gurgling stream.

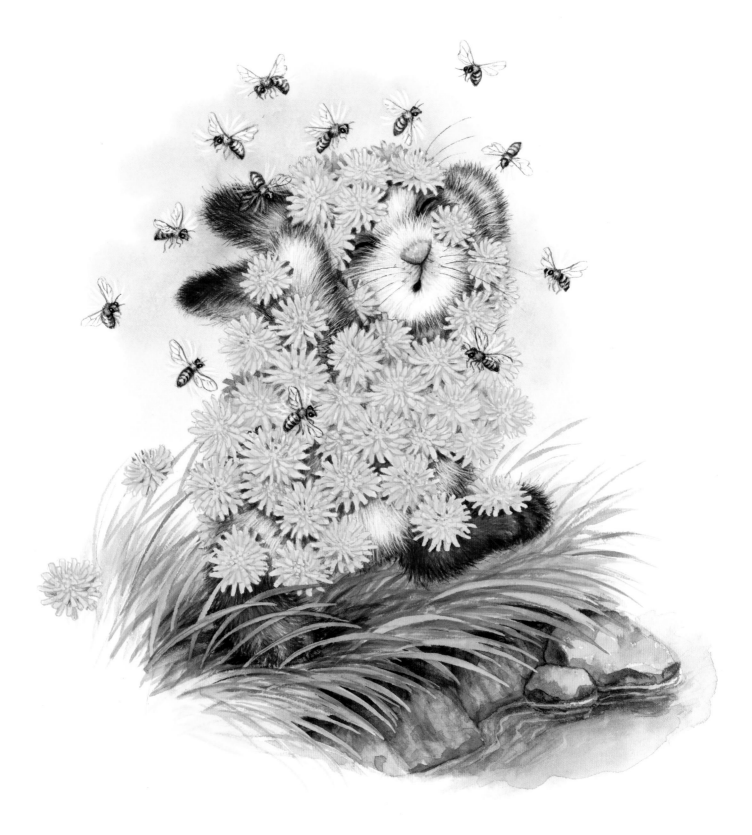

Quiet Bunny watched the yellow dandelions float away.

Nearby, a shiny green frog sat on a lily pad, catching flies.

Green is a spring color, too, thought Quiet Bunny.
Green is the color of leaves and grass, and frogs and lily pads . . .

Quiet Bunny dipped under the water. He popped back up with a floppy wet lily pad on his head. He gathered a few more and draped them over his shoulders.

"Now I am **green**!"

Quiet Bunny started down the forest path to show off his new green color. But as he hopped, the lily pads flopped, covering his eyes.

Down, down, down the hill he tumbled.

Quiet Bunny landed smack in the middle of a blueberry patch, startling a blue jay that was eating the berries.

"The blue jay is blue, the sky is blue, the berries are blue, and my fuzzy bunny paws are . . . BLUE?"

Quiet Bunny plucked a pawful of berries. He squeezed them until he was covered in juice from his ears to his toes.

"Now the rest of me is blue, too!"

A happy blue Quiet Bunny leaped and frolicked all about the meadow.

At that moment a spring shower began.

Drip...drip, drip...

drip, drip, drip, drip, drip, drip

Before long the cool rain washed away
Quiet Bunny's beautiful blue color, and the
red clay earth beneath his feet turned to mud.

Quiet Bunny wiggled his muddy red toes.

He saw the red tulips blooming around him, a little red ladybug crawling on a leaf, and a red fox padding along the forest edge.

Hmm, thought Quiet Bunny. Then—

Wheeee!

Quiet Bunny rolled round and round in the mud.

When he stood up, he wore a thick coat of red clay.

"Now I am red!"

The rain stopped and the sun shone bright and warm again. Too warm.
His coat of mud turned dry and hard.

Quiet Bunny couldn't leap. He couldn't frolic.
He could hardly move at all!

Quiet Bunny sighed. "I cannot be yellow, or green, or blue, or red," he said. "I cannot be a beautiful spring color." He shuffled over to the pond to wash off the mud.

By the time Quiet Bunny reached the pond, most of the red clay had cracked and fallen off. When he looked down at the smooth water, he saw a brown and white bunny looking up at him—and a large owl.

"Quiet Bunny," said the owl, "ducklings are yellow, frogs are green, blue jays are blue, ladybugs are red, and YOU are a brown and white bunny. That is why the spring forest is beautiful . . . .

We are all different colors, and we are all beautiful!"